Story by Joanne C. Schneider
Illustrated by John Ramirez

This book is a presentation of Pure Spirit Productions, Inc. and The JCS Collection .
Printed by arrangement with Tung Shuai Art Design Print Co., Ltd.   Printed in China.
The JCS Collection□ is a federally registered trademark of Pure Spirit Productions, Inc.

# *Claire*
## and The
## Virtue of Love

ISBN:  0-9703685-0-X
Library of Congress Card Number:  00-107060

Please visit us at www.purespiritproductions.com for more information and updates.

To the greatest treasures God has given me:

Al
Geraldine
Christine
Philip
William
Elizabeth
Dale
Tom

Claire and her pony, Swift Spirit, help a selfish boy and girl
learn to give their greatest treasure away.

Guardian angels always keep watch even if
you are behaving badly or not.  Sometimes, when
there's too much trouble for them to handle, they call for help.
And so it happened that the angels called up to Heaven for Claire
to help watch over two children who were misbehaving.

Perhaps, if Beth and Henry could have seen their angels' sad expressions, they would have stopped fighting but it was too late!  The book flew out of their hands and knocked their grandmother's treasure shelf right off the wall!  It all landed with a dreadful CRASH narrowly missing Cherub, who had been napping underneath.

The children should have tried to help their grandmother pick up the pieces of her lovely treasures, but their selfish hearts cared only about who would be blamed.

"It was your fault!" sneered Beth.
"It was YOUR fault," Henry
sneered right back!

The guardian angels looked trustingly at Claire the Pure Spirit.  She and Swift Spirit had helped so many boys and girls have a change of heart.  These children were being especially difficult.  Their hearts did not yet understand how to give their greatest treasure -- the gift of LOVE.

Would Claire play her harp to calm the children's tempers?  Would she and Swift Spirit show them a heavenly viewpoint?  The dove still glowed on Swift Spirit's saddle marking the guardian angels' distress call.  Always ready to help, Claire and her pony had come in an instant!

"Your grandpa, God rest his dear soul, gave me most of these little treasures when we were courting," she sighed as a tear glistened on her cheek. Ever so gently, Grandma placed the broken pieces in her keepsake box and carefully closed the lid. "Perhaps with a little glue and patience…" her voice trailed as loving memories filled her heart. "These gifts always remind me of your grandpa's faith in God," she added softly.

"Oh no! Not again!" thought the children, squirming and bored. "We have to listen to this same old story every time we visit!" Their minds began to wander and their hearts remained untouched.

"Well that was a long time ago and besides, you two are my special treasures now!" she said. "I know there's not much room in this old house for growing boys and girls."

"Why don't you go outside and work off some of that energy while I get dinner ready. Don't forget to keep that gate closed. We don't want Cherub wandering off. She's due to have those puppies any day now!" Grandma reminded them as she bustled off into the kitchen.

"Sorry, Grandma!", chimed the children in a hollow voice. The angels knew these words were empty. Henry and Beth didn't feel guilty. Their hearts were young and self-centered. They were more relieved in not being punished than being concerned for their grandmother's feelings.

17

Claire and Swift Spirit followed the children and their
guardian angels outside into the backyard. Claire sadly
watched as the children played.

The late afternoon spring air was cool and misty. The children passed the time with hide and seek, but their hearts were filled with questions. Claire and her heavenly companions hovered nearby.

"Why wasn't she angry?" asked Henry. "Why is she always so sweet to us even when we've caused her trouble?"

Claire stepped closer, "LOVE is the answer," she whispered to their questioning hearts.

"LOVE!" echoed the two guardian angels.

"LOVE is forgiving!" all three whispered.

"Did you say something, Henry?"
"No, did you?" he replied.
"No," she answered quietly.

Although they could not see or hear the angels, the message of LOVE began to stir in their hearts.

By now Swift Spirit was watching over Cherub who was sniffing out every possible place she might choose to have her puppies.

"I know," said Henry thinking again of play. "Let's follow Cherub. She's the only one having any fun!"

"Maybe the puppies will come tonight." Beth began to think. "Ever wonder why puppies are born? Ever wonder why we were born? Grandma says it's God's will."

Henry snickered, "You don't believe in that story?"

"Well, Grandma believes in GOD," reasoned Beth who was pleased with herself for making such a logical remark. "If it is GOD," she went on, "why does He want us to be born?"

"LOVE…LOVE…:LOVE…" Claire's message echoed through the children's hearts.
Beth gasped, "Did you say something?"
"No.  I didn't say anything!" Henry remarked.
For a moment, the LOVE in their hearts was stirred again.

Not understanding what they were feeling, Beth and Henry continued to play. "Let's have a race before supper!" Beth yelled over her shoulder as she ran through the open gate. Henry, and of course the angels, followed in a flash. Cherub was sleeping safely inside, so Swift Spirit, who loved nothing better than racing, took the lead.

After dinner, Grandma dozed in her big comfy chair as a thick blanket of fog began to surround the house.

Suddenly, Henry pointed to the backyard. "Shhhhh! Don't wake Grandma, but look! We forgot to close the gate!" Henry cried in a hoarse whisper. "We've got to find Cherub! If she's lost we'll surely be punished. I know we've caused Grandma an awful lot of trouble today," now regretting with his whole heart the broken treasures.

"That's LOVE, too," said the angels encouraging the children. "Love is putting the concerns of others before your own and being sorry for hurting someone."

Without saying a word, this time the children shared a heartfelt look.
Something was awakening deep inside them. They didn't quite
understand it, but their hearts were beating fast!

Faithfully the angels watched the children search
quietly and urgently for Cherub. The more they
looked for her, the more LOVE began filling their
young hearts. Then at last came the moment Claire
had hoped for.

Beth started, "Let's hold hands
so we don't lose each other. She
must have wandered out of the yard!"
They were determined to rescue her,
fog or no fog!

LOVE, pure LOVE
was in their hearts…

C.G.R.W.

Then through the fog a bright warm glow
appeared in front of the gate.  They began
to see clearly for the first time, the angel,
her pony, and the dove.
Henry and Beth stood listening as strains of
heavenly music from Claire's harp filled the night air.

"Don't be frightened.  We're here to help you," Claire said reading the children's
thoughts.  "We're assigned to you by your loving Father.  All God's people have
guardian angels.  Yes, your grandmother, too!"
"Who are you?" they asked in their hearts for they were too amazed to speak.

"I am Claire the Pure Spirit and this is my pony, Swift Spirit. We've come to help at the request of your angels. Guardian angels sometimes need help, especially when certain children have too much energy or feel too grown-up to believe in their loving Father in Heaven," she scolded gently.

"Listen carefully as I tell you about the most important treasure in the whole world --- It is LOVE.  And it begins in your heart!"

Henry and Beth now knew
that the angels had been
speaking to them of
LOVE all
along.

Claire's vision
showed Grandma's
treasures in a new light.
The once ordinary objects
appeared so beautiful for they were
looking at them with all the LOVE in their hearts.

"Now, look again," Claire began, "and see the LOVE with which these gifts were given."

"The eagle's strong wings are like God's love for all of his people. It shelters and protects them and lets their spirits soar!"

"This rose, too, shows God's love in the gift of life. A rose is beautiful in spite of its thorns.  The life God gives you is beautiful in spite of troubles and trials."

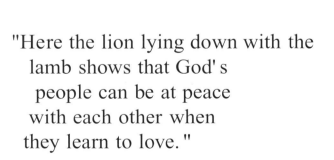

"Here the lion lying down with the lamb shows that God's people can be at peace with each other when they learn to love."

Claire spoke straight to their hearts, "You must share this most precious gift, the gift of God's LOVE."

At last Henry and Beth began to realize what their grandmother's stories had been trying to teach them all along. Together from their hearts, they prayed, "Thank you, Father. Help us to put others first."

The heavenly beings were now fading quickly with the fog as the children realized their grandmother had been calling to them. "Grandma! Grandma!" they cried as they tried to tell her about losing Cherub.

"Calm down dears! Everything is fine! Cherub woke me up and showed me her six adorable puppies! She's such a little thing. You know, she was right behind my comfy chair all the time. I guess I slept through it all. Come inside now. How would you like to name our newest treasures?"

"Oh, yes!" exclaimed the children with a sigh of relief and a heartfelt, "Thank you" to their Heavenly Father.
"Could we help fix your treasures?" Henry's words blurted out. "And would you tell us their stories again?"
Excitedly Beth added, "And, could we tell you a story too, Grandma?"
"That's LOVE!" sang the guardian angels with a heavenly voice as they followed everyone inside.

"Oh, yes!" exclaimed the children with a sigh of relief and a heartfelt, "Thank you," to their Heavenly Father.

"Could we help fix your treasures?" Henry's words blurted out. "And would you tell us their stories again?"

Excitedly Beth added, "And, could we tell you a story too, Grandma?"

"That's LOVE!" sang the guardian angels with a heavenly voice as they followed everyone inside.

"LOVE is the answer!" sang Claire as she waved goodbye.  Swift Spirit whinnied in agreement.
Soon they were joyfully floating from cloud to cloud on their return to Heaven.
With a big grin Henry asked Beth, "Did you say something?"
"Not me," she replied with a knowing look.
"But we LOVE who did!"  They both laughed with all of their hearts